Rosie The Rainbow Raindrop

Author: Jody Stockton

Illustrator: Lucas Lange

ISBN

Once upon a time, in a cloudy sky above, there was a little raindrop named Rosie. She was not like the other raindrops.

She was rainbow-colored, with beautiful shades of red, orange, yellow, green, blue, and purple. Rosie loved her unique colors, but some of the other raindrops did not.

The other raindrops made fun of her rainbow colors. They teased her and called her names "Look at her! She's so weird!" said one raindrop.

"Yeah, what's wrong with her? She doesn't even look like a real raindrop.

Rosie tried to ignore the mean things they said. But deep down, she wished she was like the other raindrops.

One day, Rosie met a cloud named Charlie. Charlie was kind and asked Rosie why she looked so sad.

Rosie told Charlie all about the other raindrops making fun of her, and Charlie listened with care. He told Rosie that being different was a good thing and that she should be proud of her rainbow colors.

Rosie felt better after talking to Charlie. She realized that he was right. She needed to stand up for herself and her beautiful colors.

So, the next time the other raindrops made fun of her, She said "I'm proud of my rainbow colors and I love being me.".

At first, the other raindrops just laughed and continued to tease her. But Rosie didn't give up. She stood up to them and told them that their mean comments hurt her feelings.

One day, a storm rolled in, and the rain started pouring down. The raindrops rushed to form a puddle on the ground, but then Rosie saw something scary.

The river had flooded, and a family
of bunnies was trapped!

Rosie knew she had to act fast. With all her might, she shone her rainbow colors as brightly as she could.

The bunnies saw her shining colors and swam towards her. Rosie led them to safety, and the bunnies were saved.

The other raindrops saw what Rosie had done, and they were amazed. They realized that being different was something to celebrate.

From that day on, Rosie was no longer bullied. She had proven to everyone that being different was a beautiful thing.

And every time it rained, the other raindrops would look at Rosie and smile, knowing that she was a hero and a true friend.

Rosie knew she didn't have to change who she was to fit in. She could be herself and still be loved and accepted. She felt proud of who she was and happy that she had made new friends.

In the end, Rosie realized that being different was what made her special. She had saved the day, and her unique rainbow colors had shone brightly for all to see.

The end.